DESPICABLE ME 3: AGNES LOVES UNICORNS!

A CENTUM BOOK 9781911460459

PUBLISHED IN GREAT BRITAIN BY CENTUM BOOKS LTD

THIS EDITION PUBLISHED 2017

© 2017 UNIVERSAL STUDIOS.

1 3 5 7 9 10 8 6 4 2

CENTUM BOOKS LTD, 20 DEVON SQUARE, NEWTON ABBOT, DEVON, TQ12 2HR, UK

BOOKS@CENTUMBOOKSLTD.CO.UK

CENTUM BOOKS LIMITED REG. NO. 07641486

A CIP CATALOGUE RECORD FOR THIS BOOK IS AVAILABLE FROM THE BRITISH LIBRARY

PRINTED IN CHINA.

ILLUMINATION PRESENTS
DESPICABLE ME3 ™

AGNES
LOVES UNICORNS!

centum

Once upon a time, there was a little girl named AGNES. She had two older sisters – the eldest was called MARGO and the other was called EDITH. The three sisters were orphans and lived at 'Miss Hattie's Home for Girls'.

Agnes
(THE YOUNGEST)

Margo
(THE ELDEST)

MISS HATTIE'S ☺
HOME FOR GIRLS

Edith
(THE MIDDLE SISTER)

7

Every night, when the girls went to sleep, AGNES DREAMT THAT A MUMMY AND DADDY WOULD ADOPT THEM. She was sure they would be adopted very soon and that the MUMMY and daddy would be nice . . .

... and have a pet **UNICORN.**

AGNES **LOVED UNICORNS.** ☺

She knew they were real. Every night she sang herself to sleep with a song she had made up, all about unicorns.

AGNES' SONG

"Unicorns, I love them! Unicorns, I love them!

Uni, uni, unicorns, I lo-o-ove them!

Uni, unicorns, I could pet one, if they were

really real . . . and THEY ARE!

So, I bought one so I could pet it.

Now it loves me, now I love it!"

After she sang this, she always had the **MOST MAGICAL DREAMS** all about unicorns.

AGNES'
TOY UNICORN

ONE DAY, AGNES' DREAM DID COME TRUE ...

just not exactly as she had always imagined.

Agnes and her sisters were adopted by **Gru**, who was a "dentist".

Gru (NOT A DENTIST)

THE GIRLS FIRST MEET GRU

THE GIRLS FIRST MEET GRU

AGNES HAS GRU'S LEG

One day, Gru took the girls to 'SUPER SILLY FUN LAND' – the most fun place on Earth! It was here that Agnes first spotted something . . . FLUFFY.

It was **LOVE AT FIRST SIGHT!** The game they were playing was unfair, but luckily Gru had a gadget that helped to level the playing field...!

GRU'S GADGET WHICH LEVELS THE PLAYING FIELD!

Agnes finally had a dad and her very own fluffy unicorn – perhaps the FLUFFIEST UNICORN EVER!

"IT'S SO FLUFFY I'M GONNA DIE!"

SHE WAS SO HAPPY. ☺

From that moment on, Agnes and Fluffy
did **EVERYTHING** together.

FLUFFY IS **HERE!**

Tea parties with Gru, **stories at bedtime . . .**

ONE BIG UNICORN
BY GRU

THIS STORY
IS ABOUT
UNICORNS TOO!

. . . and **board games** with Margo. They also slept together side-by-side every night. Agnes **LOVED** Fluffy **VERY MUCH.**

One very scary time, when the Minion Kevin was injected with PX-41, **PURPLE-KEVIN TRIED TO EAT FLUFFY!** Agnes **SCREAMED** so loudly that all the windows and Kevin's goggles shattered. Kevin dropped Fluffy. Agnes saved the day!

KEVIN'S GOGGLES **BEFORE** THEY WERE BROKEN!

NO ONE CAN COME BETWEEN A GIRL AND HER FLUFFY UNICORN!

21

As much as Agnes **LOVED** Fluffy, she loved her
family even more. So when her mummy and
daddy, Gru and Lucy, lost their jobs at the
AVL, Agnes knew what she had to do. She
held a yard sale to sell all her toys

- INCLUDING HER BELOVED FLUFFY.

FLUFFY BEING SOLD ☹

23

When the family went to visit Gru's new-found twin brother, Dru, in Freedonia, Agnes heard about a **LOCAL LEGEND**. The Legend stated that **REAL UNICORNS** roamed the nearby forest, and that if you were a maiden of the purest heart, you could find one.

AGNES AND EDITH
EVEN FOUND A REAL
UNICORN HORN IN A
PUB! **PROOF!**

Agnes knew she had a **PURE HEART** so she knew
just what she had to do . . .

Agnes and Edith set off into the forest, **DETERMINED** to find a **MYSTICAL UNICORN.** It would fulfil Agnes' lifelong dream to find and become friends with a unicorn, and Edith's more recent dream (in case unicorns did exist) of filming a unicorn and selling the video to become rich.

THIS IS HOW EDITH FEELS ABOUT THE QUEST.

THIS IS HOW EDITH IMAGINES SHE'LL FEEL IF UNICORNS ARE REAL AND SHE FILMS IT.

WHEN AGNES FINDS A UNICORN, SHE WILL GIVE IT THE BIGGEST HUG!

27

In the end, the maiden with the purest heart did find something that she knew was a unicorn in the forest.

AND iT WAS LOVE AT FiRST SIGHT.